For Miss Kelly Cassidy,
my wildflower-picking friend
from across the canal.

American Folktales for the primary grades, full of action and humor, are about America's best known and most loved folklore characters. Told in true tall-tale manner, each story has a simple plot and colorful illustrations. These delightful books, sure to appeal to beginning readers everywhere, are ideal for individualized or independent reading in the classroom or library.

Pecos Bill
And the Wonderful
Clothesline Snake

by Wyatt Blassingame

illustrated by Herman Vestal

GARRARD PUBLISHING COMPANY
CHAMPAIGN, ILLINOIS

Pecos Bill
And the Wonderful
Clothesline Snake

On his ranch away out in the West, Pecos Bill was helping his wife, Sluefoot Sue, to hang out the wash. Just then a strong wind came up and blew a pair of Pecos's pants right off the line. They sailed into the corral where Widowmaker, Pecos's horse, was half-asleep. Frightened by the pants, Widowmaker jumped 30 feet straight up in the air. He turned heels over head and came down wearing the pants.

Pecos Bill shook his head. "That horse can't wear my pants. He's not bowlegged enough."

"If we had a better clothesline, your pants would not have blown away," Sue said as she hung up a sheet, "and my clothes wouldn't get so dirty." Just then the clothesline broke, and the sheets and towels fell to the ground. In one minute they were so dirty, grass was growing on them.

The more Sue thought about the dirty clothes, the madder she got. She put both hands on her hips, and her

eyes flashed. "Pecos Bill," she yelled, "I'm telling you for the last time. I need a clothesline snake. And if you don't get one, I'm not going to wash any more clothes."

Now, as almost everybody knows, a clothesline snake is a snake with a hook on each end. It can wrap itself around a post or tree and hook itself in place. Every clothesline snake can stretch itself as long as it wants, or shrink as short as it wants, so it is always exactly the right length. It can even make little loops in itself to be used as clothespins. Clothesline snakes make the most wonderful clotheslines in the world.

"All the clothesline snakes are far away down in Snake Canyon," Pecos Bill said. "And you know our horses are afraid of snakes. I'd have to walk there."

"You won't have any clean clothes unless I have a clothesline snake," Sue said again.

Pecos Bill sighed. "Oh, all right. I'll go."

"And I'll go with you," Sue said.

So they set off. It was a long walk, but finally they reached Snake Canyon. The canyon was narrow, and the mountain cliffs on both sides were a mile high. The canyon was filled with big rocks and giant cactus plants.

Pecos Bill looked all around. "A lot of big hoop snakes live up at this end," he said.

"I don't see any," Sue said, "but I hear thunder."

Pecos listened. Far up the canyon there was a deep rumbling noise. It grew louder and louder. "That's not thunder," Pecos shouted. "That's a big hoop snake. Here it comes!"

Now, as everybody knows, hoop snakes don't crawl like other snakes. Instead, the hoop snake puts its tail in its mouth to make a hoop, and it rolls where it wants to go. This one made a hoop 100 feet high. It came rolling down the canyon, 105 miles an hour, straight toward Pecos and Sue. It knocked over a giant cactus and sent rocks bounding ahead of it.

Sue looked frightened. "Don't worry," Pecos said. He held her hand.

The hoop snake was almost on them. Just at the last second Pecos pulled Sue one quick step to the

right. Then he held her and jumped—
through the snake's hoop. This made
the snake try to turn in such a hurry
that it tied itself into 24 different
kinds of knots.

"We're safe now," Pecos told Sue.
"A tied up hoop snake can't get un-
tied before sundown."

They began to walk on into the canyon. "I'm getting tired," Sue said.

"Maybe I can find a saddle snake," Pecos said. "You can ride on it."

Well, just about that time a big saddle snake came crawling down the canyon. Now, as everybody knows, a saddle snake looks like a big snake and also like a camel. The first ten feet of this saddle snake crawled along the ground. The next ten feet were in the air, with two humps, like the humps of a camel. This made a saddle between the humps. Then the last ten feet of the snake followed along on the ground. The saddle snake did not see Pecos Bill and Sue.

Quickly Pecos got his lasso ready.
When the saddle snake raised its head
to slide over a big rock, Pecos threw
his lasso. He jerked the lasso tight
around the snake's neck.

Now this was a wild saddle snake
that had never been roped before. It

stood on its tail and spun around 100 times a second. It wrapped Pecos's lasso around its body. Pecos held on for dear life. He was pulled right into the saddle snake's saddle.

Then that saddle snake began to buck. It wriggled and turned. The

saddle part of its body slid down to the tail. Then the saddle shot back up to the head. The saddle skidded down to the middle again, but the snake couldn't shake off Pecos Bill. So it stood right up on its tail and spun 200 times in a circle.

"Ride'em, cowboy!" Pecos Bill shouted. He waved his hat with one hand and sang:

This ol' saddle snake has never been rode.

But I'm a cowboy who's never been throwed!

Wiggle and twist, you rugged reptile.

I'll sit in the saddle and smile, smile, smile.

After a while the saddle snake got so tired it could not spin. It just lay there, breathing hard. "I give up," the snake said. "You must be Pecos Bill, the cowboy."

"I am," Pecos Bill said.

"It's no wonder I couldn't throw
you," the snake said. "What are you
doing down here in Snake Canyon?"

"I'm looking for a good clothesline
snake," Pecos said. "Sluefoot Sue has
her heart set on having one. And you
know how it is when a woman makes
up her mind about something."

19

The saddle snake sighed. "I know. But all of the clothesline snakes are down at the far end of the canyon. That's a long walk."

"Sue can ride on you," Pecos told the snake. "Then we'll need another snake for me to ride."

Well, just about that time another saddle snake came wiggling out from behind a rock. Pecos started to unwind his lasso, but the saddle snake called to him, "Wait! You don't need to lasso me. If that saddle snake couldn't get away from you, it's no use for me to try. Climb on board!"

Bill got on the other saddle snake. Then he and Sue rode south down the canyon. Before long they heard a loud, rattling noise. It got louder and louder. "Look behind us!" Pecos shouted.

Through the canyon came a glass snake racing at 100 miles an hour. Right behind it was a big rattlesnake. The rattlesnake's big mouth was wide open, its fangs ready to attack. But just as it reached for the glass snake's tail, the glass snake broke itself into 50 pieces. Quickly each piece wiggled off in a different direction to hide.

"A glass snake always breaks itself into pieces when it is chased by a rattlesnake," Pecos told Sue. "That's why it's called a glass snake."

Now the rattlesnake was spinning round and round, trying to catch all 50 pieces of the glass snake. It spun so hard it broke off its own tail.

"Serves it right," Sluefoot Sue said. "It should know better than to chase that poor little glass snake!"

Well, just about that time the rattlesnake became so confused it just wiggled off down the canyon, leaving its rattle. When the rattlesnake was gone, all the pieces of the glass snake came out of hiding and began to join together again. But the glass snake made a mistake. It joined on the rattlesnake's tail instead of its own tail. When it started to crawl away, the rattlesnake's rattle began to rattle. The glass snake heard the rattle and began to run. The faster it ran, the louder the rattle sounded. When Pecos Bill and Sue last saw that glass snake, it was making a noise louder than 82 buzz saws.

Pecos Bill and Sue rode on their saddle snakes down into the canyon. Soon they passed Bell Butte, where all the bell snakes live. As everybody knows, bell snakes are kin to rattlesnakes, but instead of rattles they have bells on their tails. But unlike rattlesnakes, bell snakes are very

friendly. When the bell snakes saw Pecos and Sue riding the two saddle snakes, all the bell snakes began to ring. "How lovely!" Sue cried. "It sounds like Sunday morning!"

Bill and Sue rode on, through Pancake Pass. Here all the snakes were shaped like pancakes. Some of them had been asleep under blueberry bushes. When they awoke and moved, they carried piles of blueberries on their backs. Some carried blackberries, and one or two had syrup dripping from them. Pecos Bill shook his head. "This canyon is a strange place," he said. "I didn't know there were any syrup bushes here."

"I don't see anything so strange about that," Sue said. "Syrup bushes will grow anywhere there are pancake snakes."

So they rode on, and at last they came to the south end of Snake Canyon, where the clothesline snakes lived.

Now down in Snake Canyon these clothesline snakes all had one big problem—there never was any wet wash to be hung out. So with nothing to do, most of the clothesline snakes just lay around and did nothing. Oh, here and there one was lazily stretching itself a little bit, and another was shrinking just a little bit to keep in shape. But most of them lay coiled in the shade of rocks and bushes.

"A lazy lot!" the big saddle snake muttered.

But just then Sue called to Pecos, "Look! Over there!"

Off to Pecos's right, one young clothesline snake was stretched like a rope between two tall cactus plants. Up and down its long body, small birds were sitting. Some were whistling softly. Some of the birds were sleeping, their heads tucked under their wings. The clothesline snake was swaying gently back and forth, singing:

Rockabye birdie

  on your clothesline snake.
When the wind blows,
  your swing won't break.
There's no danger
  that you will fall.
The clothesline snake
  takes care of it all.

Sue clapped her hands happily. "That clothesline snake is so pretty and gentle! And yet—it looks so sad. Even its voice is sad."

Well, about that time the young clothesline snake shook its body so all the birds flew away. Then it unhooked one end of itself from one cactus and the other end from the other cactus. It wriggled over beside

Sluefoot Sue. The clothesline snake
had tears in its eyes. "You'd be sad
too, ma'am," the snake said, "if you
were a young clothesline snake who
wanted to work but had nothing to
do. I don't want to be lazy like most
of the other snakes around here. I
want to work. Oh, I hang out for the

birds sometimes. But they can rest anywhere. A young clothesline snake needs to have clothes hung on him to be useful."

"Well," Sue said, "that's why I'm here. We have lots of laundry because Pecos works around the ranch and gets dirty all the time. But I've told him I won't wash any more clothes unless I have a clothesline snake to help."

With that, the clothesline snake jumped straight up in the air. It shrank until it was only two feet long and landed in Sue's lap. "Let's go to the ranch!" it cried. "I want to be your clothesline snake!"

But now all the other clothesline snakes were crawling around. They were interested in what was going on. All the clothesline snakes wanted to go back to the ranch with Sluefoot Sue and Pecos Bill. They crawled over one another, shouting, "Take me! Take me!" Or, "I'm the biggest!" Or, "I'll work and try the hardest!"

"But we can't take you all," Sue said. "There just isn't room for all of you to hang up. We can only take one. But which one will it be?" she asked Pecos.

"We'll have to run a contest to pick the right one," Pecos Bill said.

He told the snakes, "All right.

Now each one of you pretend to be a clothesline. There are lots of clothes on you. Show Sue why she should choose you to be her clothesline.''

All the clothesline snakes began to stretch themselves between whatever they could reach—cactus plants and

rocks and tree limbs, and even each other. But some of them had been lazy for so long that now they could only stretch a little bit. Some were too fat to shrink. Some were so far out of practice they couldn't hook onto anything.

While Sue and Bill were watching the contest, the young clothesline snake slithered down from Sue's lap. It fastened its tail to a tree limb. Then it made loops around a small bush, and three bigger bushes. Then it stretched out to a fourth, still bigger, bush, and then onto another tree limb.

As it did, it sang:

> I'm not the prettiest
>   clothesline snake,
> but the line I make
>   will never break.
> And when Sue's laundry
>   is clean and dry,
> and she'd like to swing,
>   I know that I
> can fasten one end
>   to the limb of a tree,
> let the other end hang,
>   loose and free.
> At the lower end
>   I'll form a ring,
> where Sue can sit
>   to swing and swing.

"And I *do* love to swing!" Sue cried. "That's the clothesline snake I want, Pecos."

"You've made a very good choice," Pecos said. "I don't think these other snakes really want to work, or they wouldn't be so lazy. They wouldn't be any fun, either."

So Sluefoot Sue and Pecos Bill
took the young clothesline snake home
with them. And from that time on,
Sue had a clothesline that was always
exactly the right length. Pecos Bill always had clean clothes to work in.
Widowmaker was never frightened by
Pecos's pants blowing into the corral.

And when the laundry was dry and put away, Sluefoot Sue and the young clothesline snake would happily sing and swing, and swing and sing. And sometimes Pecos did too.